It's time for swimming lessons!

Don't fret, there's nothing to worry about.

Soon, you'll be ready to . . .

1, 2, 3, Jump!

Lisl H. Detlefsen

Illustrated by
Madeline Valentine

ROARING BROOK PRESS
New York

The first thing you need to do is put on your suit.

No, not that type of suit.
A *swim*suit, silly!

Some swimmers also wear a cap.
Oops—not again!
A rubbery, stretchy, waterproof,
colorful *swim* cap.

Goggles are helpful, too.
Seriously?
You think *those* goggles are going
to help you in the pool?

Okay, you're finally ready to jump into swimming lessons.

When you arrive at your first lesson, you'll meet the other students and the teacher.
Your swim teacher will be an extremely good swimmer.

But not a goldfish.

Or the Loch Ness Monster.

Or a mermaid.

You don't need a fancy fin to swim!
Though if your lesson goes well,
you might get to put a pair of
flippers on your feet.

Your swim teacher will begin by teaching
you some important safety information.

Like no running
around the pool.

And stay on the wall
when it's not your turn.

And don't use your favorite
stuffed animal as a flotation
device.

Now, 1, 2, 3,

JUMP!

You're not ready yet?

No, the water isn't so cold it will turn you into a kidsicle.

You'll get used to it.

Yes, that smell is totally normal for a swimming pool.
It's the chlorine added to keep the pool clean.

No, that *shlurping* sound isn't a sea creature trying
to suck you into its mouth.
It's just a filter.

Let´s start by getting comfortable in the water.

Hey, get your blankie out of there!
That´s not what I meant by "comfortable"!

Try dangling your legs in the shallow end.
Fish won't nibble your toes!

Aren't you going to get into the pool?
Don't think about the deep end just yet.
Instead, think about trying on those flippers!

You´re just not ready?

Maybe you could practice blowing bubbles.

No, not like that!

Just put your lips underwater and
hum your favorite tune.
Hmm, hmm, hmm, HMM!
Well done!

Time to put your head underwater.

No, the swimming pool
is not home to sharks.
Or alligators.
Or shark-a-gators.
Even in the deep end.

Thanks to those handy swim goggles, you can put your face in the water and see for yourself.

A little farther . . .

Almost there . . .

SUPER!

Now, you can get into the pool, right?
1, 2, 3 . . . **JUMP!**

What?
You still need more time?

Let's move on to floating.

Relax and let the water hold you up.

First on your back.

Then on your tummy.

Time to get those legs into the action!

I know you're excited about the flippers, but first you should learn the flutter kick and the dolphin kick.

Flutter, flutter, flutter.

Great kicking!

Now, let's have some fun. Who can make the biggest splashes?

Wow! You've really got the hang of it!
But you do realize you need to get *into the pool*
to really learn how to swim, right?

Seriously, you *can* do this!
Your swim teacher will catch you, I promise.
Just one big jump and then everyone can
try out the flippers, okay?

Let's count together.

1...
  2...
    3...

Hooray!

You did it!

I knew you had it in you.

Flippers for everyone!

For my favorite mermaids and shark-a-gators, especially Eryka, Natalie, and Brycen —L.D.

For all the little swimmers out there, especially Solly —M.V.

Text copyright © 2019 by Lisl H. Detlefsen
Illustrations copyright © 2019 by Madeline Valentine
Published by Roaring Brook Press
Roaring Brook Press is a division of Holtzbrinck Publishing Holdings Limited Partnership
175 Fifth Avenue, New York, NY 10010

mackids.com

Library of Congress Control Number: 2018955661
ISBN: 978-1-62672-681-9

Our books may be purchased in bulk for promotional, educational, or business use. Please contact your local bookseller or the Macmillan Corporate and Premium Sales Department at (800) 221-7945 ext. 5442 or by email at MacmillanSpecialMarkets@macmillan.com.

First edition, 2019

Printed in China by RR Donnelley Asia Printing Solutions Ltd.,
Dongguan City, Guangdong Province

1 3 5 7 9 10 8 6 4 2